MW00947885

The Adventures of Chi-Chi the Chinchilla

by
Ekaterina Gaidouk

Copyright © 2020 Ekaterina Gaidouk.

All rights reserved. No part of this book may be reproduced, stored, or transmitted by any means—whether auditory, graphic, mechanical, or electronic—without written permission of the author, except in the case of brief excerpts used in critical articles and reviews. Unauthorized reproduction of any part of this work is illegal and is punishable by law.

This is a work of fiction. All of the characters, names, incidents, organizations, and dialogue in this novel are either the products of the author's imagination or are used fictitiously.

ISBN: 978-1-7165-6106-1 (sc)
ISBN: 978-1-7165-6107-8 (hc)
ISBN: 978-1-7165-6105-4 (e)

Library of Congress Control Number: 2020917614

Because of the dynamic nature of the Internet, any web addresses or links contained in this book may have changed since publication and may no longer be valid. The views expressed in this work are solely those of the author and do not necessarily reflect the views of the publisher, and the publisher hereby disclaims any responsibility for them.

Lulu Publishing Services rev. date: 09/22/2020

To the children.

In the deep forest, among the vast mountains of Chile, there used to live a young chinchilla by the name of Chi- Chi.

Chi-Chi was well-loved by his family and friends. He was young, happy, and playful.

He liked running through the forest with his friends and eating with his family and, above all, he, as all chinchillas do, loved raisins—the prized rare treat usually eaten by humans.

What Chi-Chi didn't like was work!

Many times he left chores and schoolwork undone.

As nocturnal animals, his parents worked night and even day to build a home, clean it, and collect food—only sleeping in the early hours of the morning.

But Chi-Chi enjoyed taking a nap after a good meal, and he usually did so without finishing his chores!

Often, his father was responsible for collecting Chi-Chi's small share of food, hay, and twigs.

Chi-Chi's father wished his son would help more, but he thought it was best to lead by example. Many times he would collect a few extra tree branches to give to the neighbors who were struggling to build their homes. "You see, my son, a little kindness goes a long way," explained Chi-Chi's father to him.

But of course Chi-Chi did not see or understand why anyone would work extra, so he continued to play more than help.

One day when Chi-Chi was playing outside with his friends, a furious rainstorm overtook the small chinchilla village.

Inside their home, Chi-Chi's mother was running from window to window on the lookout for Chi-Chi and his father. She was relieved to see Chi-Chi coming home, but there was no sign of his father!

Only in the morning did Chi-Chi's father return, and he carried a full bag of food and hay he had collected, but he returned very wet.

"The rain was so strong that I was forced to hide inside a log on my way home," his father said. "I'm wet, but I think that I'm all right."

The next morning, Chi-Chi's father fell very ill. He could not get out of bed.

Chi-Chi's mother called Chi-Chi to the kitchen, where she was preparing soup for his father.

"Chi-Chi, your father is very ill. I need you to go into the town of Piaola to collect raisins for him from the people who live there. Raisins are our most precious food and medicine, and if he eats the raisins, they will help him get better."

"Yes, Mother, of course I will go," Chi-Chi replied, knowing that raisins were the best medicine as well as the tastiest treat but very difficult for chinchillas to find. Only humans had them.

As his mother stirred the soup, she continued. "I'm giving you a map with directions on how to collect the raisins. Here's a canister for you to put them in. Please, Chi-Chi, be careful, and make sure to follow the directions."

Chi-Chi nodded in agreement as he ate his breakfast.

Chi-Chi had heard about the town of Piaola from his friends. He knew that it was up on the very top of the mountain and that the people who lived there were friendly and kind.

People had lived in the town of Piaola for many years and were accustomed to giving treats to the chinchillas who made the far journey up the mountain.

In fact, since chinchillas had the finest fur and most playful personalities, they were considered a sign of good luck, especially if they showed up on the doorstep. Many kids and adults alike put little cups of raisins on their doorsteps in hopes of seeing a chinchilla.

"Take your time, ask for help, and look at the directions," Chi-Chi's mother reminded him as he hurriedly packed his backpack and ran out the door. He wanted to help his father as quickly as possible. He knew that time was of the essence, so he did not bother reading the map or the directions his mother had given him.

Instead, Chi-Chi followed his instincts and the stories of his friends who told him to head straight up to the peak of the mountain.

Chi-Chi ran, ran, and then ran some more.

I should be close to Piaola by now, Chi-Chi thought as he ran up the mountain.

Finally, he slowed down and began to walk through what seemed like a vast forest. Suddenly, he came upon a trail of raisins!

Chi-Chi became excited as he decided to follow the trail, eating each raisin that he came upon. *This must lead to many more, so it is okay if I eat them,* he thought.

20

The trail led him inside a log! When Chi-Chi went into the log, he found a small pile of raisins at the other end! And although he was very full, he decided to eat more and only put a couple in his backpack.

After he had finished, he decided it was time to return home. But as he tried to climb out of the log, he found out that he was stuck! He pushed and pushed but could not get out. Only his head fit through the log!

Oh no, Chi-Chi thought. *How will I get out?*

Just then a wise turtle was passing by.

"Please, Mr. Turtle, help me!" Chi-Chi cried out.

Mr. Turtle looked at Chi-Chi and the log and smiled. He decided to help Chi-Chi get out. So he started pulling on Chi-Chi's ears, and *pop!* Chi-Chi flew out. But so did the few raisins that he had put in his backpack instead of the canister his mother had given him.

The wise turtle knew about the magic trail of raisins and the tricky log that trapped anybody who was too greedy to share the hidden treasure.

"You see, my young friend, when you only think of yourself, you simply get stuck in one place," said Mr. Turtle.

"Yes, I see now," said Chi-Chi. "But Mr. Turtle, I'm lost. The map my mother gave me flew out of my backpack with the raisins. Can you help me get to the town of Piaola?"

"Yes, I can. I will give you a map with directions, if you can beat me in a race," said Mr. Turtle.

"All right. That seems simple enough," said Chi-Chi.

"The first one to cross the finish line at the only palm tree in this forest wins," said Mr. Turtle.

"You can either follow this trail on the ground," Mr. Turtle said as he pointed to the tiny, brown path right next to him, "or you can look at the directions inscribed on the map hanging on the trunk of that oak tree in the opposite corner." Mr. Turtle pointed to the dark oak tree that was clearly in the opposite direction of the trail.

He added, "We both start when I say go."

"On your mark, get set, *go!*" said Mr. Turtle

Chi-Chi did not want to waste time going in the opposite direction of the trail, nor did he want to waste time reading the directions when a clear path was right in front of him. So he raced off in the direction of the trail.

This is easy. Mr. Turtle must be getting old and not thinking clearly, Chi-Chi thought as he ran as fast as his little legs could move him.

He ran and ran and ran some more, following the path Mr. Turtle had pointed out. Finally, he saw the palm tree in the distance so he ran even faster. With no sign of Mr. Turtle behind him, Chi-Chi thought he was about to win.

Suddenly, he saw, beneath the palm tree, across the finish line, Mr. Turtle!

Chi-Chi could not believe his eyes as he finally reached the finish line. "Oh no!" he exclaimed. "This is impossible! How could you have beaten me?"

Seeing that Chi-Chi was clearly out of breath, Mr. Turtle simply held up the map that he had taken down from the oak tree. As Chi-Chi looked closer at the map, he saw that the path he had chosen was a circle!

"You see, my young friend," explained Mr. Turtle, "if you had taken the time to read the directions, you would have seen that all you had to do to beat me was to run across the bridge behind the bushes to reach this palm tree. But instead, you followed the path that seemed clearer but turned out to be longer since it simply took you in a circle."

"I understand now," Chi-Chi said, disappointed in himself. "I simply rush through many tasks without thinking there may be a better way."

Mr. Turtle came up to the crouching Chi-Chi and handed him a copy of the map to Piaola. "Here you go, my young friend. You have learned the lesson, and I believe this may help you."

Chi-Chi looked up and took the map to Piaola from

Mr. Turtle.

"Thank you, sir. I really do appreciate it. But how will you ever find your way to Piaola without a map?" asked Chi-Chi.

"I have been to Piaola many times and do not need a map to reach it," answered Mr. Turtle.

"Thank you, sir, for everything," said Chi-Chi as he carefully looked at the map and read the directions. The map clearly showed the special trail Chi-Chi had to follow to reach the town of Piaola.

The instructions below the map explained that, since most people went indoors after 10:00 p.m. and took away the bowls of raisins they had put out during the afternoon, it was best to reach Piaola before nightfall. Rarely did a chinchilla show up to claim the prized treat, but when one did, it was considered extremely fortunate, for it took a special type of nocturnal animal to make the journey.

I must hurry, Chi-Chi thought as he put the map in his backpack and ran toward the hidden path.

The dirt path that he came upon was full of twists and turns, but Chi-Chi was careful to pay attention and not stray away from it.

Finally, he saw the small town of Piaola ahead.

He raced toward the village, but as he reached the first doorstep, he realized that it was dark! The sun had set!

He ran from house to house in hopes of catching a person's attention or finding a bowl of raisins. But everybody was inside already, and all the bowls were empty!

What will I do now? My father needs the raisins to get better, Chi-Chi thought as he sat down on the last doorstep of the small village. He did not want to let his family down but knew he could not stay the night in the village since his mother was expecting him home.

As he sat in silence, Chi-Chi heard a whimper. He walked toward the sound and soon found a little girl crying on her doorstep holding a broken necklace.

Chi-Chi could tell that she was very sad that something of great importance was broken. He thought of how he felt when he lost his raisins and his map and decided to cheer the girl up by doing a little dance.

38

You see, chinchillas are playful animals who love to move around and dance. In fact, Chi-Chi was known to be a great dancer.

As he jumped and twirled in front of the little girl, she stopped crying and began to smile and clap at the dancing chinchilla. The smile encouraged Chi-Chi to continue his show. Then, as he jumped and spun on his tippy toes, he lost his balance and—*boom!*—fell on his bushy tail.

Laughter filled the air as the little girl ran toward Chi-Chi to help him out. Not only did she forget the broken necklace, but now she was jumping and dancing with Chi-Chi!

The little girl's parents heard the commotion coming from the front porch and decided to see what was going on. When they came out, they could not help but smile as they saw their young daughter dancing with the friendly chinchilla. Chi-Chi was definitely enjoying the attention!

When they stopped dancing, the parents called Chi-Chi and their daughter over. "My daughter, you have made a new friend. You see, happiness comes from simple things," said the mother as she hugged her daughter.

"As for you, little chinchilla, we thank you for your kindness and realize you must be hungry, so we brought you a bowl of raisins," the little girl's father said to Chi-Chi as he put down a bowl filled with the precious treat.

Chi-Chi expressed his joy by jumping up and down around the family, filling the air with laughter once again.

Chi-Chi packed his canister with many raisins, eating only a few himself. He patted his stomach to show that he was full and pointed toward the path he had to take back home, for he knew he must return to his family.

The little girl came up to Chi-Chi and hugged him. "Thank you for your kindness, and have a safe journey home," she said.

Chi-Chi looked back one more time at the family and waved goodbye before he began to skip happily along the trail toward his home.

He stopped several times to check that his raisins were safely kept within the canister, and he reviewed his map to make sure he had not strayed from the trail.

Finally, Chi-Chi arrived home. He burst through the door and ran into his the arms of his mother, who had stayed up waiting for her young son.

"Chi-Chi, I was so worried about you," said Chi-Chi's mother as she covered Chi-Chi with her kisses.

"Moooommmm," said Chi-Chi, "I'm okay. Don't worry. Look at what I brought!"

Chi-Chi emptied the canister onto the kitchen table.

There were so many raisins that some even spilled on the floor!

His mother was overcome with pride and joy as she looked from the raisins to Chi-Chi. She said, "You must be very hungry. Would you like me to prepare a stew for you with the raisins that you brought?"

"No thanks, Mom. I already ate enough. May I take some up to Papa?" answered Chi-Chi.

"Of course you may," she said as she cleaned and put several raisins on a plate for Chi-Chi to take up to his father.

Chi-Chi walked up the stairs into his father's bedroom, where he found him sleeping but clearly not well, since even in his sleep he was coughing. He carefully put the plate of raisins on the nightstand and walked away.

"I hope these help you, Papa, and I'm sorry for not helping you when I should have. Please get better. Good night," said Chi-Chi as he quietly walked out of the bedroom.

Late the next evening, Chi-Chi went downstairs to eat breakfast, and he saw his father at the table!

"Papa! Papa! You are well!" cried Chi-Chi as he ran to hug him.

"Yes, my son, I'm feeling much better. I ate the raisins you left for me late last night. They have definitely helped me, because I feel reenergized and well," said his father.

"But tell me, Chi-Chi: how did you get so many raisins? The people of Piaola are known to put out only a few raisins a day, especially since they rarely see a chinchilla and they do not want to waste the treat."

"It's like you always told me: a little kindness goes a long way," said Chi-Chi as he finished his breakfast and ran off to school with his backpack full of books and his heart full of joy.

Chi-Chi could not wait to tell his friends about the valuable lessons he had learned on his first adventure from home.

His parents could not help but smile as they realized their little Chi-Chi was as full of surprises as he was full of life.